First published in the Hebrew language in Israel in 2003 by Kinneret, Zmora-Bitan
First published in the UK in 2023 by Green Bean Books
c/o Pen & Sword Books Ltd
George House, Unit 12 & 13, Beevor Street, Off Pontefract Road, Barnsley, South Yorkshire S71 1HN
www.greenbeanbooks.com

Paperback edition ISBN 978-1-80500-003-7
Harold Grinspoon Foundation edition ISBN 978-1-80500-007-5

Designed by Ian Hughes
Edited by Julie Carpenter and Sammy Marcus Leventhal
Production by Hugh Allan

Printed in China by Printworks Global Ltd, London and Hong Kong
1023/B2358/A4

Green
Bean
Books

www.greenbeanbooks.com

A Beautiful World

Written by
Yael Gover

Illustrated by
Paul Kor

Translated by
Gilah Kahn-Hoffmann

Green
Bean
Books

The sky is black

It's dark all around . . .

but I've found an amazing paintbrush!

What's missing?

What can I add?

Which colors should I pick?

Maybe . . .

I'll think for a minute,
or maybe for two . . .
what else will be
in my world?

No crashing waves can
reach the top of the hill.
The summit is dry, so it's a
place where I could stand.
I think I'll call it . . .

The smell of the flowers wafts through the garden all day, but then night falls. Even flowers need to rest. And so I decide to invite Mister . . .

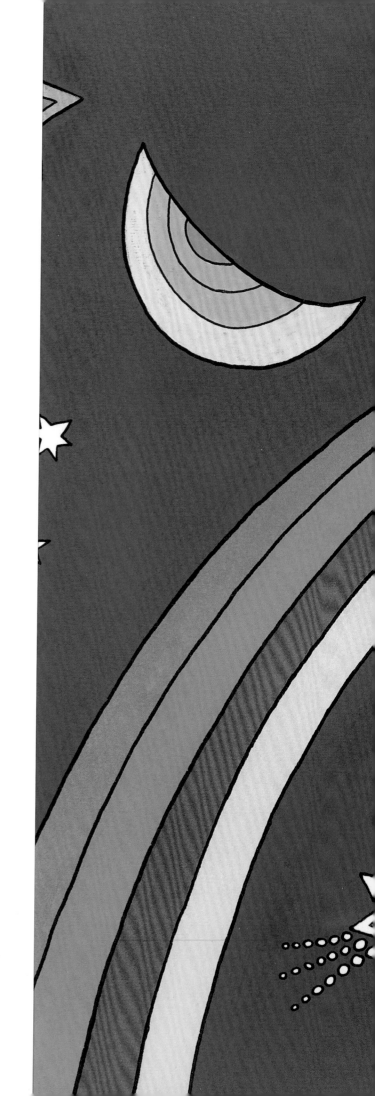

I have a beautiful world.

It's almost complete.

But wait! What's missing?

Who will swim in my sea?

Who will walk my paths?

Who will soar through

the sky?

I'm missing creatures that

swim, run and fly.

I'm missing . . .

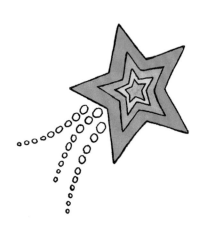

Now tell me, who will dive

into the waves?

We need some great

swimmers.

What do you think we

should have? Yes –

The sea is a little crowded
and choppy.

There's no more
room here, so now's the
time to draw something
somewhere else.

What's still missing?

What do we need?

Maybe . . .

My picture looks almost
done.

Is there a sky?

Yes!

And a sea?

Naturally!

Do we have creatures?

We do!

And plants growing?

We have those, too!

Now my painting
is unfurled.

Look, it's such a lovely . . .

YOU!